I0549841

2023 Best Short Stories
Riversong Contest

Edited by Neela Tudurí-Kłepfisch

RIVERSONG
BOOKS

An Imprint of Sulis International Press
Los Angeles | Dallas | London

ISBN (print): 978-1-958139-24-0
ISBN (eBook): 978-1-958139-25-7

Published by Riversong Books
An Imprint of Sulis International
Los Angeles | Dallas | London

www.sulisinternational.com

Contents

Preface

This is the second volume of the annual River-song Short Story Contest. I am proud to edit this volume of winning stories for publication. We had peer 30 short stories submitted in a wide variety of genres. Many were excellent, and our judges struggled over the final 3 or 4 to fill out our limit of no more than six stories. There were so many splendid works, and I look forward to next year's submissions. It is encouraging to see the number of fine writers in a digital age of short texts and attention spans.

Thank you to my fellow Contest Judges of the Contest:

- Sheri Addison, freelance editor

- Anthony Holmes, Director of Publishing, Sulis International Press

- Mira Innes, literature blogger

- Mark McFaddyn, editor, Sulis International Press

- John Sparks, editor and reviewer, *Historical Fiction Review*

The winning stories include genres of literary fiction, poetry, AI-generated and edited, contemporary fiction, poetry, and fantasy—from writers as young as 17 and as old as 65, from all parts of the globe.

Congratulations to Mikel, Admi, Endy, Suzanne, Tiffany, and Susanne, from all of us here at Sulis International Press and Riversong Books.

Neela Tudurí-Kłepfisch
Miami
July 31, 2023

Showpiece

Mikal Dobrovski[1]

"Hey, friend, what's up?"

Shaun looked up from where he was working near the corner of his house. Walking down the sidewalk was a heavy man in his 30s or 40s, wearing a jogging suit and tennis shoes, looking a bit like he hadn't left the 1980s. His salt-and-pepper hair was cropped short—Shaun could imagine the smell of pomade. The man smiled

---

[1]Mikal Dobrovski is a promising voice in the world of literature. Born in 1999 and raised in Austin, Texas, he has always had a passion for writing. After completing his education in literature, he worked as a freelance editor while writing shorts stories. He has published in local magazines and online blogs, gaining positive attention for his fresh, vibrant prose, and captivating storytelling. Currently, Mikal is working on his debut novel, a contemporary fiction and slice-of-life work about a homeless man making his way through life in Austin. You can find him on Twitter and Instagram at @chasgalberts19995.

and spoke again. "You just moved in last week, didn't you? Welcome to the neighborhood!"

Shaun straightened up, and shifted the pipe wrench to his left hand. "Thank you. Yes, just last week. Making some repairs, getting the house in order."

"My name is Ben—Ben Nabors. I live down at the corner." He pointed back the way he had come.

"Shaun Pantas." He strode across the small front lawn, wiping his hands on his trousers, and extended his right hand, still holding the wrench in his left.

"What are you working on?" Ben asked, nodding at the house.

"The main water pipe is leaking, and the valve is broken, so I'm trying to repair it. Having trouble getting the old fittings off."

"Yeah, these houses are pretty old. I imagine the fittings are pretty corroded if it hasn't been maintained." He leaned in towards Shaun. "It was no secret the Idantes didn't keep up the house. Did minimal stuff on the outside, but the inside was a mess! But I guess I don't need to tell you that!" he said, pretending to give him a nudge without touching him.

"Yes, it was pretty bad."

"Last time we were there, a few weeks before they left, we saw the staircase railing had come loose! Not to mention some missing base-boards, open electric sockets…my wife and I said to each other, 'oh, how sad for the next owner!'" Ben flinched a bit, and laughed. "To each his own, though, right? It was their house." He hesitated. "I figured you'd be inside work-ing, not outside, I guess."

"Well, I enjoy all kinds of handiwork. It's one reason I bought this house. Came out for a change of pace—I have been working pretty hard on the inside, though. Making progress. The inside is where we live, after all." Shaun smiled.

"True, true. Well, I need to continue my walk," Ben said, "If you ever need any help, let me know—I am pretty handy myself—and we'd love to see what you have done to the place when you're ready for visitors!" He paused again. "Not that I am inviting myself. We've just always thought the place could be such a beautiful home."

"Oh, yes, of course. I'd love to have guests—when it is in better shape. I'll let you know. En-joy your walk!"

Shaun stood for a few moments watching Ben lope down the sidewalk. He turned and went back to work.

*

Three weeks later, Shaun was standing on the sidewalk at the end of the walkway that came down from the front porch, gazing back at his house and his latest effort. He had repainted all the porch framing and wooden flooring, having replaced any wooden planks that had rotted or split from long neglect. He still needed to repair the concrete steps that led up to the porch. And he wanted to replace the double front doors. He envisioned two heavy oak doors with beveled glass windows up high—enough to let in light and set off the beauty of the wood, but not big enough for people to see inside.

He heard a door open behind him. He turned his head and saw the neighbor who lived across the street, Amie Nicolais, coming towards the street to check her mailbox. He had met her a week or so ago, just for a moment. She was an attractive young woman in her late twenties, Shaun guessed. She was just out of college and lived with another young woman named Frieda. Shaun hadn't met Frieda yet—she was always at work, according to Amie.

Amie looked up as she reached the mailbox. "Hi, Shaun, how are you?"

"Doing well, Amie. And you?"

"Good." She pulled the mail from the mailbox and tucked it under her arm, then turned her attention back to him. "Wow, the porch looks great! You have such a talent! I noticed the driveway last weekend. Looks much better—and lining it with red-stone was such a nice touch. You are going to put the rest of us to shame!"

Shaun laughed. "I don't know about that, there are plenty of fine homes in this neighborhood. But thank you. I do love this sort of work."

"Well, it shows! Frieda and I were just talking about how good it looks—the inside must be spectacular!"

"Well, I am working on it. It has a great floorplan, and it is a wonderful place to live."

"Have you done anything with the living room fireplace? The Idantes had let the wood decay, and some of the surrounding marble was broken. Such a shame—it looked as if it had been beautiful at one time."

"It is a beautiful piece of work—built to be the focal point of the parlor," replied Shaun. "I want to restore it to its original state. It had a carved mantelpiece, with ornate designs, but it is badly damaged now. I am going to try to duplicate it."

"Well, let us know when you finish! We would love to see it."

"Of course. Can't let my handiwork go unseen, can I?" He smiled.

Amie smiled back. "Have a great day!"

She turned away. Shaun nodded. "Thanks. You too."

He turned back to his handiwork.

*

A week later, Shaun was on the roof with a to-do list. First, he was going to replace all the broken shingles. Then, he would clean all the upper story windows—they were filthy. Next, he'd sand the window frames and the mullions. That would probably take a whole day. Once all that was done, he could repaint. He also needed to examine the shutters and decide if they needed to be replaced, repaired, or just sanded and repainted. The ones on the first story had needed some minor repairs and repainting, which he had done.

He made his way with care across the roof to the first window, which was set in a dormer facing the street. He examined the window and frame. A voice sounded from below. He turned his head, and saw an elderly man standing below on his lawn. Mr. Oldford was a widower who took walks around the neighborhood three times a day. Everyone knew him, though no one seemed to know his first name: it was as if his first name was "Mister." He walked with a slight stoop, leaning on a cane with each alternate step. He often mentioned how much he loved to walk. It was clear, however, that talking was his real love.

Shaun turned around with care and squatted down on his haunches to stabilize himself on the slope. "Hello, Mr. Oldford. What's that, you say? I can't hear too well up here."

Mr. Oldford lifted one hand to shade his eyes from the sun and peered up to the roof. "I said, 'how is the renovation coming along?'" The shouting seemed to tax his energy.

"Going well, thank you!" replied Shaun, louder than necessary, but he hated having to repeat himself over and over, a common occurrence when conversing with Mr. Oldford. "I want to get the roof and dormers repaired before the end of the week. We're supposed to get some rain next week."

"Yes, yes, I heard that. Are ya goin' ta work on the gutters? They look pretty good t' me!"

"Yeah, I think they are in good shape. I cleaned out the insides and scrubbed the outsides."

There was a long pause. Mr. Oldford seemed to be catching his breath, looking up and down the upper part of the house. Shaun waited patiently, hoping Mr. Oldford would get bored and move along. Finally, he seemed to regain his energy. "Well, it's lookin' great!" He paused to cough. "You're the talk of the neighborhood with the fine work yer doin'."

Shaun smiled. He was proud of his skills. "Thank you. I enjoy the work."

"Well, it's great what you're doing t' this house. Such a shame what the Idantes' had let it come to. That kitchen was such a wonder. My wife, 'afore she died, said it was the best kitchen she'd ever seen: a large island in the middle, a built-in cutting block, a wine closet, the hangin' rack for pans 'n' glasses 'n' such. I think the original owners had it all custom done!"

"Yes, I take pride in restoring an old house to its intended beauty."

"Never heard the end of that kitchen from her," he chuckled. "She went on 'n' on about it." He stopped, and seemed to drift off into the past. His head dropped. Shaun said nothing, waiting.

Finally, Mr. Oldford seemed to give a slight shiver and return to the present. He looked up again. "Well, I won't bother ya any longer. Gotta go walk: I love my walks, ya know!" He leaned on his cane and shuffled to turn away.

"Love t' see the kitchen when ya finish. Have a good day, young man!"

"Thank you, Mr. Oldford." He rose with care and turned back to the dormer. When he was sure Mr. Oldford had time to shuffle back to the sidewalk, he turned and watched the old man make his way down the street. Once he was out of sight, he turned his attention back to the window.

*

An ambulance sat in front of the house, its lights spinning and flashing. A crowd stood around, some on the sidewalk in front of the ambulance, some standing on the manicured lawn. Others stood in the street. A few had ventured up close to the steps of the repaired and painted porch. It was decorated with plants, some in pots strategically placed around the porch, others in hanging baskets. Two hand-crafted rocking chairs, an upholstered chaise lounge, and a small table with candles and a tea set completed the scene. Out of place on this front porch was a police officer in full uniform, standing near the front door, arms crossed, watching the crowd.

Ben Nabors and his wife, Millie, were standing beside Amie.

"So you didn't hear or see anything?" Ben asked Amie.

"No, I didn't," she replied, one arm hugging her opposite side while she held her other hand up near her mouth. She seemed stunned. "I just heard—I heard the ambulance pull up, and I came out to see what was going on."

"Do you know him well?"

"Not really. I mean, I talked to him almost every day, briefly. He was always outside working on this place. But—not much…talk about anything…much. Anything important."

"Yeah, me too. Never any lengthy conversations. I wonder if he hurt himself working on the house—fell or something?"

"Oh, I hope it is nothing serious. I was afraid maybe someone broke in and attacked him, with the house being so beautiful. He's obviously wealthy to spend all that money on the house."

Millie spoke up. "Oh, have you been inside?"

"No, I never have. You?"

"No. We have heard it is just beautiful. That it even puts the outside to shame." She turned toward a man standing nearby. "Hey, Dave! Didn't you tell me about the marble and wood staircase he built inside?"

Dave moved closer to the three. "Yeah. Heard it is remarkable. Wonder what's going on?" They all shrugged and nodded. "Well," continued David, "I had hoped to see it someday. I hope he's okay."

"Oh, you haven't seen it?" asked Ben.

"No, I've never been inside, though he said he was going to invite me when he got more of it finished."

The four neighbors stood for a moment. Amie broke the silence. "You know, he has been living here for seven months. Has anyone seen inside? I keep hearing people say how great it looks."

There was silence for a moment.

"Well, *someone* must have been inside," Ben said. "He was a friendly guy, not a loner. Always willing to stop working, to have a chat."

Millie took up Amie thought. "But did he ever invite any of you inside?"

At that moment, Mr. Oldford crutched his way over to them. "Hello, neighbors. Tragedy, eh?"

"Do you know what happened?" asked Millie.

"No," answered Mr. Oldford, "but those medics been in there a long time, and not a one has come out yet, except right at first when they came t' get the gurney. In my experience, that spells bad news."

"Were you ever inside the house, Mr. Oldford?" asked Millie.

"No, never was. We had plans to have tea on the back patio he'd re-done, but never got 'round to it. He was a busy boy, workin' on this beaut'. Loved that kind of work—real good at it," he finished, nodding up towards the magnificent edifice.

A commotion at the front door caused them all to turn quickly. The door flew open and a cluster of medics and police officers could be seen inside. The room behind the door was lit, but the light was moving, as if from flashlights.

Some bustling resulted in a gurney being maneuvered out the door, carried by four medics, with another medic holding a bag up with a hose coming out and going into the bundled body on the stretcher. The neighbors tried to get a glimpse, but the body was bound up and covered, even his face, so much so that they couldn't see anything in the darkness. The medics slid the gurney into the back of the ambulance, slammed the doors, jumped inside, all with surprising quickness. The ambulance sped off with lights flaring and siren blaring.

Clumping boots on wood caused the crowd to turn back towards the porch. Two police officers came out, closing the door behind them, and headed down the porch. "Ok, people, nothing else going on here. Go back to your homes."

"What's happened?" someone yelled.

The officer looked in the direction of the voice without stopping. "Not really sure, but he's where he needs to be now. Call the hospital later."

"Was it an accident while he was working on his house?!"

"A heart attack?"

"Did someone attack him?"

By this time, the police were at their car. The one on the passenger side opened the door, paused, and looked out at the crowd. "No signs of an intrusion. We don't know anything yet. Go home, call the hospital later." He got in the car and they drove off.

The crowd stood still in a silence that contrasted with the noise that had been going on for the last hour or so. A low murmuring grew as people began talking to one another again. They began to move off in groups or singly.

Ben, Millie, Amie, and Mr. Oldford stood in the yard. Amie turned and looked at the house. Ben was staring at the ground. Mr. Oldford coughed. "Well, I guess that is that. Didn't look good to me. Was alive, I guess. For now. I seen this before, though." He stared at the ground, shaking his head.

Millie turned and looked at the house. "I don't think they locked the door."

Ben looked up with a start. "What?"

She turned to face him. "I don't think they locked the door."

"Let's go check," Amie said, already heading towards the porch. Millie was right behind her, and Mr. Oldford turned and began a slow hobble towards the porch as well.

Ben stood his ground. "Wait…"

He hesitated for a moment, then followed. By the time he caught up to them, Amie had her hand on the ornate doorknob. The oak door was even more beautiful up close. "Do you think this was *hand*-carved?" she asked.

She turned the knob. "It isn't locked." She opened the door with care. It swung with a smooth and silent motion, though she could feel it was quite heavy, but well-balanced on large oiled hinges. The other three crowded up into the doorframe. The room was dark: they could see nothing.

"I wonder where the lights are," whispered Millie.

Amie took one step inside, then felt along the wall beside the door. Light appeared, but it was dim, as if it was coming from inside an old, yellowed lampshade. Outlines and shadows were all they could see of the entryway: yet they could tell it was a large room, with a staircase on one side going up to the second story and a balustrade at the top running perpendicular to the stairs. The outline of three upstairs doors could be seen behind the railing. There were archways leading into other rooms on either side, darkness beyond. In front of the group was another, larger archway, leading deeper into the house, also dark. In the dim light, this room appeared to be an awe-inspiring introduction to Shaun's masterpiece.

"There must be other lights," Ben said. He pushed past the others and headed towards the staircase along the left wall.

"Maybe we shouldn't do this," Amie murmured.

"It was your idea," Ben said over his shoulder. He was peering along the wall between the stairs and the archway.

"I know." She looked down. "But I feel weird now."

"Oh, it's okay," Mr. Oldford said. "He's our neighbor, we all know him. This house is his baby—he'd appreciate us checkin' it out and lockin' up."

"Found them," Ben said. They heard clicking of switches. One. Nothing. Two. Nothing. Three…

They all squinted and blinked as the entryway lit up with a bright light. It was coming from a large cluster of bulbs—part of a magnificent chandelier hanging at the center of the entry. Their eyes began to adjust.

Millie gasped.

The wooden floor at their feet was a mess. Not only had it been stripped of its lacquer, but it was scarred and splintered. Beginning near the right-hand archway, a long, twisted groove ran for ten feet towards the central archway, as if someone had dragged a heavy object across the floor. A layer of dust lay on everything, disturbed by many footprints. The wallpaper on the walls was peeling. A thick oriental style rug lay in the center of the entryway, but it was threadbare in places, curled up on one corner, and had a large dark stain near the front as if some dark, viscous substance had been spilled on it.

Now that their eyes had adjusted, they could see that the stairway railings were in a similar state. All the wood needed repair. The stairsteps were bare, worn wood, with a dip in the center of each step from years of people walking the stairs. Three or four of the steps were missing entirely; black, yawning maws. Even the chandelier, so magnificent at first glance, was damaged, missing several bulbs, and hanging at a slight tilt.

"Oh…my…God," Amie said.

Ben, standing over by the wall facing them, laughed—a strange, out-of-place sound—and said, "Well, I guess he hadn't gotten to working on this part yet. Thought I don't remember it being this bad when the Idantes moved out."

Mr. Oldford coughed. "I suppose he's been busy with the rest o' the house…"

Millie headed to the archway on the right. "Now that we are here, we might as well see what he *has* been doing."

Ben stepped to intercept her. "Wait, Millie. Maybe we shouldn't. Feels like…intruding."

She reached the archway, feeling around the side for another light. "We are checking his house to make sure all is okay while he is in the hospital."

"Well…" started Ben.

"Smells kinda funny in here," Mr. Oldford said, "like…"

"Yes," Amie said. "Maybe he left a stove on or another door unlocked. He won't mind. He's such a nice guy." She followed Millie.

Ben looked at Mr. Oldford, who turned to follow the women. "Okay. If I remember right, this is the parlor."

As they all reached the archway, Millie found the light, and the room lit up. Again, they stood in silence and gazed at the sight before them. It was the same: a floor with heavy damage, peeling wallpaper, torn curtains—but the dust was less disturbed here. From the center of the ceiling hung a long chain with bare wires protruding from the end. The light came from a floor lamp near the front wall, missing its shade.

But what caught their attention was the large fireplace in the center of the far wall. The wood mantel was weathered; cracked, with numerous splits and dents. Though they could tell it had ornate carved designs along the front, they were so damaged it was hard to tell what the designs were. A layer of thick dust was visible on the top of the mantelpiece from where they stood. The sides and the floor-piece of the fireplace were made of marble, but so dirty that the four neighbors could not perceive the original color. White? Gray? Green? Much of the grout between the large squares of marble was missing. The left bottom corner of the floor-piece had a large chunk missing, as if something heavy had been dropped on it. The inside of the fireplace was black, from thousands of roaring fires too large for even this fireplace—and never cleaned. Inside the fireplace, part of a metal grate protruded from a thick pile of ashes, which spilled out onto the marble and onto the wood floor.

"Oh, my," Amie said. "The fireplace needed work when the Idantes were here, but this is terrible. How could Shaun, of all people, let this happen?"

"That damage isn't just from neglect," Ben replied. "Something has happened since he bought the place."

"Mebbe," Mr. Oldford said, "but the whole *house* can't be this way. I wanna see the kitchen." He hobbled back through the archway and then turned right, passing underneath the entryway balcony.

The others followed. "It does smell strange in here," Millie said, sniffing. "Rats?"

"I am going upstairs to check the bedrooms," Ben said.

Millie nodded. "I'll check the other rooms down here."

Amie followed Mr. Oldford. She reached the door of the kitchen and Mr. Oldford turned on the lights.

"Oh, oh. Betty would be so upset. It's good she can't see this. She loved this kitchen."

The room was gutted. Yet it did not appear as if someone had removed cabinets with purpose or a plan to begin a restoration. It seemed more like vandals had made their way through in a whirlwind of destruction. The lower cabinets, which enclosed the sink, had been yanked away from the wall a bit, and the entire structure stood at an angle protruding into the kitchen, some of the wood broken or smashed. The tile floor was missing about half of its large tiles.

Parts of the wallboard were gone, exposing rusted and broken pipes and electrical wiring, some of the latter looking as if rats had gnawed on them. A refrigerator stood in its nook, but the door was standing open with no interior light, and they could make out the remains of rotting food inside.

Mr. Oldford shuffled through the dirt and dust, kicking pieces of wood and tile out of his way has he headed to the back door. Amie turned and looked through at the dining room to the right, through another archway. Though the lights were not on in there, the light from the kitchen showed it to be in similar condition. The dining room table was missing a leg and had fallen down on that side, sloping towards Amie like a ramp. A chandelier was lying on its side near the opposite wall. She brought her gaze back towards the kitchen and spotted the missing table leg, broken near the top, lying near where she stood. She stepped back into the kitchen.

Mr. Oldford had opened the back door and stood looking out. "Hmph," she heard him exclaim, then he turned and began to make his way back through the debris.

"Same?" she asked.

"Yep. Or worse. Looks like a garbage dump. I s'pose it could be from all his outside work, but the gardens are bare and the trees and bushes and grass are all dead. The back patio is piled with junk."

They heard someone in the entryway and headed back.

Millie was standing in the entry, near the far archway. "It's just unbelievable. How could this house get like this? How could he *live* in it?"

"How could he make the outside so beautiful and *thoroughly* ignore the inside? It makes no sense," Amie replied.

They heard a noise above them and looked up. Ben had come out of one of the upstairs rooms and was walking along the balcony back towards the stairs. He looked down at them. "Whole upstairs is like this. I can't believe someone so talented could live in this."

He reached the top of the stairs and started down. A cracking sound came from under his feet. Ben swayed and grabbed for the railing.

"What's that?" Millie yelled.

"The step's giving way," he said.

"Be careful!"

He placed his foot onto the next step with care: the toe first, lowering to the heel, then more weight. Another crack—louder this time. He began to move more quickly. Rending wood and the splintering sounds grew louder. Amie and Millie screamed. Ben leaned upon the railway to take some of his weight off the stairs, but it began to give way as well. Mr. Oldford stumbled backwards to avoid the falling balustrade, and tripped and fell against the wall near the left archway. The wallboard caved in as if it was made of cardboard.

"Mr. Oldford!" Amie ran towards him.

"Ben!" Millie screamed. The entire structure of the stairs began to pull away from the wall and into the entryway. Ben jumped the last set of steps. The entire stairway collapsed. He landed on the wood floor and came down to his knees, hands splayed out on in front of him. The floorboards beneath him cracked, one broke in half, and he fell with his right arm extending through the hole below the floor level. He yelled in pain. The noise was loud, and the dust was thick in the air.

Millie had scrambled backwards to avoid the falling staircase. She slammed back into the side of the archway from where she had just come. The upright beam of the arch behind her splintered and broke in two where she struck it, as if it was made of Styrofoam. She slid to the floor with a grunt.

Amie, having grabbed Mr. Oldford and held him up, looked over at the archway. "Millie, it's coming down!" Millie scrambled across the floor towards Ben. The archway began to crumble in slow motion, and then it too collapsed in another cloud of dust and dirt, leaving rotted and broken wooden beams hanging in all directions.

They were all coughing. Millie helped Bento stand, while Amie held Mr. Oldford's arm. They stumbled towards the front door. Mr. Oldford's cane was gone. Ben's right arm was bleeding from a number of scratches and cuts.

Another cracking and splintering sound came from above and behind the four. They turned in unison and saw that the balcony above the kitchen archway was beginning to sag. Creaking, splintering, and then roaring filled the room as the magnificent balcony slowly bent in its middle, then began to break into pieces. The whole of the balcony structure tilted towards them, pulling away from the far wall to which it had been anchored. They turned and flung their arms over their heads. The noise was deafening, like a head-on crash of train boxcars: rending wood, splintering metal, groaning beams and shattered glass.

When the noise subsided, they helped each other up and looked at each other in horror, covered in dust and debris. The entryway looked like a junkyard. The dust in the air made it unbreathable. They coughed. The silence was ominous after all the noise, as if a cacophonic orchestra had just hit the final note of one movement, and was holding quiet, just waiting for the conductor to swipe his baton through the air to begin the powerful notes of the next movement.

Then, in the deep recesses of the house, they heard creaks and groans—some upstairs, some downstairs, some below the house.

"Let's get out of here now!" Ben yelled. He turned to the door and reached for the knob. They heard something crash from somewhere in the house, followed by more splintering sounds.

"It's stuck!" Ben wrestled with the door. Amie grabbed the handle below the doorknob and helped Ben pull. The door came loose with a jerk, and both fell back into Millie and Mr. Oldford, all four collapsing in a heap. The momentum of the door caused it to slam into the far wall, and a crack splintered up the wall, then another sideways. The top hinge of the door gave way, and the door fell to the floor with a crash, just beside the four of them.

They helped each other up, and almost carrying Mr. Oldford, they scrambled through the front door just as the lintel fell. The sounds of destruction increased behind them as they ran out onto the porch, down the stairs, and out into the yard. When they reached the sidewalk, they collapsed on the grass, with coughs and heavy breathing.

The sounds of creaking and crashing and breaking became louder. The four neighbors rolled over and watched. The beautiful porch began to collapse, beginning with the roof. The vertical beams, as if under tremendous weight, bent and then cracked. The roof of the porch collapsed in on itself. This caused the main roof of the house to careen forward. The dormers, so restored and painted with painstaking care, were trembling as if in an earthquake. One of the windows shattered, spewing glass outward. The chimney, on the right side of the house, was swaying back and forth. Bricks began to fall, and then, finally, the entire chimney collapsed down into itself and spilled over onto the roof, cracking the tiles and bouncing down onto the ruins of the porch and then came to rest on the front lawn.

A terrific groan emanated from the structure, and the roof over the center of the house appeared to buckle, then collapse inward, an imploding house. When the collapsing sections of the roof reached the outer walls, those last upright structures trembled, bent, and then collapsed inward.

The motion stopped. Small creaks, the tinkling of glass, and the shifting sounds slowly subsided, until there was silence.

Ben, Millie, Amie, and Mr. Oldford sat looking at the pile of rubble that had once been the showpiece of the neighborhood, the handiwork of a fine artisan, and the envy of all. A mountain of splintered wood, broken stone, bent pipes, and a rising cloud of smoke and dust was all that was left.

A.I. in the Jungle

Admi Freoman[1]

A young man is far from home,
alone in a foreign land, with an uncertain future
He longs for the comfort of his own home,
but all he has is the wind that blows.

At war, the young man is alone in an unfamiliar land.
Lost and afraid, with no comrades to huddle with,

---

[1]Admi Freeman is a 15-year-old student living in Arizona.
His grandfather fought in WWII, and this is his tribute.
Adam loves reading historical fiction about the World
Wars, poetry, and experimenting with what AI can do.
This poem was AI-generated, based on concepts and
themes entered by Admi, and then edited and expanded by
him.
He has been writing verse since he was seven years old.

he looks up at the tall buildings
 and hears the rustle and bungle of leaves.

His fears double in the heart of the town.
The streets are unfamiliar, and the language is strange.
He feels trapped in a world that is deranged.
Every day is a struggle, and every moment is a range
emotions that leave him feeling estranged.

He walks the streets with a heavy heart,
watching people pass who are worlds apart.
He feels like he's playing a part in a story
that's tearing him apart.

He remembers the days of his youth,
filled with laughter and love, the sweetest truth.
Now he's here, searching for proof
that he can survive against the ruthless.

With every step, he tries to find his way
to a place where he can finally stay.
But for now, he's lost and can only pray
for the strength to make it through another day.

A.I. in the Jungle

Alone with no comrades, he lost his way.
He runs from the town while it is still day.
The forest beckons, "come to me,"
He reaches the trees at the final ray.

Alone in the jungle, so dark and deep,
with strange sounds and sights that make him creep.
The trees are so tall, the leaves rustle and weep.
In this heart of darkness, his fears do heap.

The silence is broken by a rustle in the brush.
He feels the fear as it makes him rush.
The sounds of the jungle, like a haunting hush,
in this wild world, he feels like helpless mush.

He tries to find his way out, but the forest is dense.
The strange sounds and sights only add to his suspense.
He walks slowly with caution and defense
and hopes that he'll find a way
with some common sense.

He hears strange sounds from all around,
a rustle in the bushes, a snap on the ground.
His heart beats fast, his senses astound.
In this jungle of war, no peace can be found.

He dreams of home, of a life so pure,
of love and laughter, of times so sure.
But here in the jungle, his fate is obscure,
alone and lost, his spirit demure.

The eyes of the jungle watch him with might.
He feels their gaze in the dead of the night.
The fear takes over with all its might
as he tries to survive with all his sight.

He longs for the comfort of his own bed,
but here in the jungle, he feels like he's dead.
The strange sounds and sights fill him with dread
as he searches for a way out with all his head.

He dreams of the sunsets on the beach,
the sound of the waves within his reach,
the warmth of his family's love, a lesson to teach.
But for now, he's just a stranger, an outsider to beseech.

The animals of the jungle are everywhere.
He hears their growls and feels the scare.
He tries to run, but doesn't know where.
In this jungle of death, he feels like a snare.

A.I. in the Jungle

He longs for the taste of his mother's cooking,
the sound of his father's voice,
never mistook for anything else,
a symphony of love, never shook.

But for now, he's just a wanderer, a book to
overlook.
He prays for the strength to make it through
and hopes that one day he'll start anew
in a world that's bright, with skies so blue.

But for now, he's alone in a jungle, so true.
He walks for hours with no end in sight.
The jungle is vast, and he's losing his might.
He wonders if he'll make it through the night
and hopes that he'll find some relief in the light.

He hears a sound in the distance
 so far and hopes that it's not something bizarre.
He walks towards it with a trembling heart
and hopes that it's not a dangerous scar.

He reaches a clearing with a river
so wide and feels a sense of relief deep inside.
He drinks some water and takes a deep sigh
and hopes that he'll make it with a few more
strides.

He rests for a while with a calm mind a
and feels like he's left his fears behind.
He knows that he'll have to keep looking to find
a way out
of the jungle with all of his grind.

He dreams of the day when he'll be back home
and how he'll be welcomed with open arms to
roam,
of the love and laughter that he'll never disown
and how he'll never be lost in the jungle alone.

The war rages on, but he fights alone.
A battle of his own that he has sown
in this jungle of death, he has grown,
a warrior at heart, forever unknown.

Forest

Endy O'Hara[1]

Thomas loved to take walks in the forest. He's been doing it since he was a child. For almost 70 years. He knew every tree. Every animal. Every path like old friends. The forest was dense and dark. Towering trees that seemed to reach to the sky. The air was thick with the smell of damp earth and decaying leaves. Every sound was muffled by the heavy canopy above.

On this day, Thomas walked deep into the forest. Farther than he had ever gone. It was the Summer Solstice. So much daylight.

He traversed areas never seen. After a few hours, the trees and underbrush seemed differ-

---

[1]Endy O'Hara is a budding author and literature major at Mayfield University. He has published a number of short stories in various online journals and university publications. He is currently working on his first novel, a fantasy set in medieval France.

ent from the familiar. Taller. Thicker. More close.

The trunks appeared close in around him. The sunlight was blocked out. It was hazy and dim. He found it hard to see more than a few feet in any direction. It wasn't the weather because the forecast was for clear skies.

This had a different feel. Not weather. Not the time of year. Not the time of day. Or maybe he was imagining it because he was traversing new land. Still, this felt dark and ominous. A thick layer of dead leaves and branches crunched beneath his feet. Every step felt like walking on a pile of desiccated bones.

The only other sounds were the rustling of leaves and the occasional snap of a twig underfoot. It was so quiet that he could hear his own heartbeat pounding in his ears, and he couldn't help but feel like he was being watched.

The trees themselves began to take on a sinister quality, with gnarled branches and twisted trunks that looked like they were reaching out to grab him. He would come up with a start, staring at the trees and trunks, which remained still until began walking again. He had been in this forest so many times over the years, what was going on? Strange shadows flickered across the ground, and he couldn't help but feel like something was following him, just out of sight.

Again, every time he stopped and looked behind him, there was nothing but silence and stillness.

Was he beginning to get dementia? Surely that didn't come on so quickly? Was he having a heart attack? There was no pain or even discomfort.

He continued to push through the forest, his sense of unease grew stronger. Every rustle in the leaves or crack of a branch made him jump, and he couldn't shake the feeling that he was being watched by something dark and malevolent.

Thomas considered turning around and going back. But that was silly. He walked this path several times a week, almost every day, for decades. If there was something untoward in this forest, he would know by now. It was probably tricks of the light and the breeze.

The further he went, the more he began to feel suffocated. This wasn't worth it. He turned and retraced his steps, but now everything looked unfamiliar. But he couldn't have taken the wrong turn, he had encountered no forks in the path.

He had been going for some time, and it felt like he should have come to the fork that led across a little stream and up to his home. At first, he thought time was playing tricks on him, but he noted the sun was setting. He had not brought a flashlight or anything with him. He never did. Why should he for a well-known stroll in familiar woods?

Now he began to get worried, and wondered if he should find shelter before it got too dark. Everything should clear up in the morning light. Could he find an overhang of rocks? Perhaps he could build a lean to? No, there wouldn't be enough light left.

He was getting more anxious. He stumbled through the woods, tripping over roots and dodging low branches. It began to mist, and then a light rain fell. Of course, he thought.

All at once, he stumbled into a small clearing, he stopped, staring at an old cabin standing in its midst. It was weathered and worn by years of use and neglect. The structure was small and squat, with a sloping roof and creaky wooden walls that were stained by the elements. He had explored this forest extensively. How had he never seen this old place? Of course, he didn't know where he was, perhaps there was a part of the first he had never discovered for some reason.

Apparently, this decrepit cabin was not vacant. He now saw a thin wisp of smoke curling from the chimney. The place still had an air of abandonment about it. It seemed as though the forest had claimed the cabin as its own, surrounding it with dense undergrowth and over-hanging branches. Whoever had lit the fire had never done anything to clean up the exterior.

He walked closer, standing before the stairs, looking up at the porch. The door was made of heavy timber planks, and a rusted iron latch held it shut. There were no windows on the front of the cabin. He stepped over to one side of the cabin and then another, spotting only a few small, dusty panes on either side.

Back at the front of the cabin, he noted the porch that ran along the front was sagging, its steps almost entirely rotted away. The roof overhang dripped with rainwater, the droplets pattering softly onto the worn wooden planks beneath.

He stepped up carefully onto the porch, plac-ing his feet on the stair supports, not trusting the rotting wood steps. He knocked at the door and waited. Twice. Maybe that wasn't smoke from the chimney. Possibly, just water vapor from the rain. In any case, it would serve as better shelter than anything else he could find now that it was dusk.

He lifted the latch and slowly opened the door. It creaked with age and decay. The interior was no more welcoming than the exterior. It was a single room inside. For a moment, he wondered if he would find a dead body in the ragged bedclothes, but there was no one—dead or living. The walls were lined with rough-hewn timber, and the furniture was old and worn. A potbelly stove stood in the center of the cabin, its blackened metal sides pockmarked with rust.

A few flickering candles provided the only light in the dimly lit interior. So someone was here. Or had been here recently. The air was musty and smelled of damp earth, with the occasional whiff of woodsmoke wafting in from the chimney. There has been a fire in the fireplace recently, though it was now just smoldering blackened wood and ash.

Tom was struck by how odd the cabin was. It was old and rundown, but there was something strange about the decor that he couldn't quite put his finger on. The walls were adorned with strange symbols, and the furniture seemed to be from a different era.

Despite its obvious neglect, there was something strangely alluring about the cabin. It was as if the worn and weathered exterior held secrets and stories that only the forest could tell. It was a place of solitude and reflection, a reminder that even in the wilds of the woods, there was always the possibility of finding a home.

"What do you want?"

Tom jumped and turned abruptly and saw there was an old woman standing in the doorway. She had a basket full of some sort of vegetables, or perhaps fruits. Her clothing was best described as rags, sewed together roughly.

"I apologize for entering your home. I thought it was vacant. I'm lost," Thomas said. "I just need a place to rest for the night."

The old woman's eyes softened. "Very well," she said. "It is quite inhospitable out there at dusk. I'll make you some tea."

She set the basket beside a wash tub.

He watched as she fiddled with the fireplace and added a couple of logs. As the old woman brewed a pot of tea. With the fire rekindled, the cabin was warm and dry, despite its small size and clutter. Without speaking, she filled a kettle with water from a bucket and placed it on an iron rod over the fire. Taking two cups out of a cabinet, she dropped a sachet of tea in each from a nearby container. By the time she put the tea away and washed the vegetables, the teapot was whistling. Thomas stayed quiet. He wondered how long she had lived here, but did not feel like she wanted the silence broken.

She took a rag for a potholder and lifted the kettle, filling each cup with steaming water. She sat down across from Thomas, placing one cup in front of each of them.

"Thank you for your hospitality," Thomas said, after taking a tentative sip. He did not know the flavor, but it was woodsy and smokey. "I don't know what I would have done without you.

The old woman smiled sadly. "I know what it's like to be lost in the forest."

Thomas sipped his tea and looked around the room. There were shelves filled with jars of herbs, an old rocking chair, and a pile of books in the corner.

"Do you live here alone?" he asked.

The old woman nodded. "I've been living in this cabin for as long as I can remember," she said. "I have everything I need here."

"How did you come to live here? I have explored this forest for many years of my life, but never found it."

"I'm not surprised. It occupies…it…it's a unique meadow and cabin." She stared into the distance for a moment, then returned his gaze and began speaking.

Her name was Maeve, and she had always felt more at home in the quiet of the woods than in the bustle of the city. Much like Tom. As a young woman, she had spent long hours wandering the trails that crisscrossed this forest, learning the secrets of the trees and the animals that lived within them.

"Then," she continued, "many decades ago, I found myself lost. It surprised me because I thought I knew the forest like the back of my hand."

Thomas a sat up. "Yes! This is what happened to me, too."

Maeve said that eventually, just before dusk, she found herself in this clearing with the old cabin. She was strangely drawn to it, and did not feel anxious or afraid. Her grandfather had told her about an old cabin in the woods where he used to spend summers. She assumed this was it. Drawn to an old cabin deep in the heart of the woods. As she neared the cabin, so long ago, she saw a wisp of smoke from the fire. She knocked, and when there Sed no answer, she entered. The fire was just smoking ash. She spent the night there, but no one ever appeared. Who had lived here, or lit the fire that morning, was a mystery to her.

Despite its age and wear, Maeve had fallen in love with its quiet simplicity and the sense of history that clung to its walls. Perhaps this was her long-dead grandfather's place, though nothing inside reminded her of him, nor were any of the belongings familiar to her.

She decided to stay for a day or two. She cleaned that place up a bit, found a nearby well. She found herself happy, and decided to stay.

Her family sand friends would be worried, sure-ly, and perhaps a search team would find her eventually. It seemed a bit odd to her that she did not care about their concern or worry.

She dug a small vegetable garden, and gath-ered firewood to keep her cozy during the win-ter months. She spent her days reading (for there were many books in the cabin), writing, and wandering the woods, observing the natural world around her and finding inspiration in the beauty of the forest.

Despite her solitary existence, Maeve was never lonely. She had learned to listen to the whispers of the trees and the songs of the birds, and they were her constant companions. The wildlife in the woods knew her well, and she had even befriended a few of the more curious creatures, like a playful fox that would some-times come to visit.

Maeve's life was a simple one, but it was filled with joy and wonder. She had found peace in the woods, and the old cabin had become a sanctuary where she could be close to the earth and the creatures that called it home. She had no desire to return to the world beyond the woods, for she had found everything she needed right there in the heart of the forest.

"I believe it is my destiny to live here until I die." She waved her hand absently. "Whenever that may be."

It was a strange tale, and Thomas was not quite sure what top make of it. All this time alone—surely it had affected her mind.

Thomas finished his tea and thanked the old woman again. He admitted to himself that this was a peaceful place, and the woman's life was intriguing, but he needed to get home. But not in the dark.

"Would you mind if I stayed here for the night?" he asked. "I don't't think I can find my way home in the dark."

The old woman smiled. "Of course," she said. "I have an extra mattress in the loft. You may sleep on it.

Thomas climbed the ladder to the loft and fell asleep almost instantly.

*

The next morning, he woke up to the sound of birds chirping outside. He climbed down the ladder and found the old woman in the kitchen making breakfast.

"Good morning," she said. "Did you sleep well?"

Thomas nodded. "Thank you for everything," he said. "I think I can find my way home now."

"The storm is pretty bad, but perhaps it will let up." For the first time, Thomas heard the pounding rain. How did he not hear it in the loft?

"And you must eat something first. Here," she said, loading a wooden plate and setting it on the table. "There is also tea."

The plate was piled high with eggs, fruit, and bread. It did smell good. "Okay. Thank you so much, you are quite kind."

After they finished eating, he stepped onto the porch and saw that it would not be wise to find his way back. The rain was still coming down hard, and there was a fierce wind. He was glad for shelter, but anxious to get back. Something just didn't seem—

"Quite the storms we get here," her voice said, right beside him. He had not heard her come out onto the porch.

He shook his head. "It is strange because I have rarely seen rain and wind like this at home, just beyond the forest."

She nodded and stood watching the rain. "This is an interesting meadow."

Maeve told him that when the weather is inhospitable, she reads, cleans up, and sips tea. Thomas found a book about World War II aircraft, and spent most of the day reading it, keeping one eye on the rain and wind. It did not let up.

Maeve prepared a lunch of boiled vegetables and egg sandwiches. Still, the rain came down. They continued to read. A few times, Thomas asked her questions about her life or the cabin, but her responses were short and vague. She had seemed talkative before. Was he prying too much now?

Eventually, Maeve stood and said, "it does not look like the rain is going to let up today. I will make us some dinner, and you can sleep here again. Perhaps in the morning, the sun will be out."

Thomas was frustrated at her lack of concern for his need to get back home. But she wasn't wrong. It would be unwise for him to attempt a trip back in this weather.

In the morning, Tom woke up feeling groggy and disoriented. He couldn't remember much about the night before, but he felt as though he had been drugged. Dragging himself up, he saw through one of the dim side windows that the sun was indeed shining. Blinking, he turned around to see Maeve at the fire with a pan, making breakfast.

"Good norming, Thomas. I'm preparing a wonderful breakfast."

He felt like he was suffocating. He stumbled to the door and out under the porch, hoping to get some fresh air.

He was horrified to find that the woods around the cabin had changed. The trees were blackened and twisted, their branches gnarled and reaching towards the sky. The sky was a sickly yellow, and the air was thick with an acrid smell that made Tom's eyes water.

He didn't know what could've happened or what was going on. With panic setting in, he sat out down the path at a run. As he stumbled through the woods, he had no idea how to get back to the familiar woods near his home. He tried to retrace his steps from two days ago, but it seemed as though the woods themselves were conspiring to keep him trapped.

His heart left as he saw a bit of sunlight up ahead. Racing down the path, he found himself in a little meadow. An old, decrepit cabin sat within the simple meadow, a wisp of smoke escaping from its chimney.

Has he skidded to a halt, he saw Maeve in the doorway, holding a plate of food. Her face was expressionless.

"Breakfast is ready, Thomas."

Looking Through Me

Tiffany McNamara-Smith[1]

What a horrible day. Christy kicked at a clod of dirt that was on the sidewalk and kept walking. Of course, all her days were bad, but this one was worse than most. She just wanted to get home, turn on the radio, and lay on the bed and chill.

During last summer, she had been eagerly awaiting high school. But after a month of school, she realized it was no different from junior high. Yes, it was a different school, different teachers, and more talk about ("you'd better prepare yourself for college!") But it was still the same attitudes, the same environment, same shit. Today was worse than most. In English,

[1] Tiffany McNamara-Smith is a teacher and counselor living in Johannesburg, SA. She works with orphaned and adopted teenagers and young adults. She has been writing short stories and novella based on her experiences. This is her first published story.

47

Mr. Lutton accused her of cheating. They had taken a quiz and then exchanged papers to grade them. She was daydreaming and didn't mark any wrong, so he accused her of trying to help Stephanie get a better grade. *I wouldn't help that bitch do anything, let alone get a better grade!* She tried to explain to him, but he didn't hear a word she said, as if she wasn't even talking. He just kept asking her why she'd take such a risk to help out a friend. *Friend? Hah!*

And if that wasn't bad enough, at lunch she had finished eating and stood up with her tray, only to be bumped by someone walking by. She lost her grip on the tray, and it clattered onto the table, spilling dishes and utensils and leftover food. *Everyone in the cafeteria was looking and laughing at me.* It was like one of those bad teenage movies. The guy who bumped her said he was sorry, but he was laughing, too. *I know he did it on purpose. Jerk! Just 'cause I told Jennie what he said about her!*

To top it all off, when she opened her locker at the end of the day, a bunch of her textbooks fell out of the top shelf and slammed her forearm, causing her to drop all the books she was carrying. *And Annie and her "gang" just happened to be walking by, and they all burst out laughing and looking at me like they hated me, which they do, but who cares anyway…*

She turned the corner and headed down her street. She lived less than a mile from the school, so she always walked home because she lived so close. *Half a block more and I can turn up my music and forget this whole stupid day!* At least her Mom wouldn't bug her about it. She never asked about school. Usually, that bothered Christy, but today it was a benefit. What a horrible day!

*

She tossed her book bag on the couch and went into the kitchen.

"Is that you, Christy?"

"Yes, Mother," she said. *Who else? We're the only ones who live here.* That is, since she got kicked out of her last school and Dad left them and mom found a new job here in this godforsaken town. She went to the refrigerator and took out a Coke, grabbed the bag of potato chips out of the pantry, and headed down the hall to her room.

"Christy?" her Mom called again.

"What?"

"Don't forget to pack your suitcase tonight."

Christy stopped. Crap, she thought, I'm supposed to stay with Dad over the weekend. She hated the obligatory once-every-two-week visit.

He hates me. When I got caught at school with drugs the last time…what he said I was to him… Maybe I can get out of it somehow—

"Christy, did you hear me? Your Dad is picking you up after school tomorrow, so you've got to pack tonight."

"Do I have to go, Mom? I wanna skip this weekend."

Her Mom appeared at the door, tucking her shirt in. "Now, Christy, you know your Dad wants to see you. And you should want to see him too. He *is* your father."

Yeah, that's why he treated me the way he did. Yeah, I know weed is illegal. I know carrying a knife is illegal. But that school was a mess. You either joined in or you got beat up every day. She never wanted to be that way, but the few friends she had….it didn't matter. She did regret what she did, and now she was paying for it. And now she doesn't do drugs, got away from that school, and was trying to do better. But nothing changed. And Dad had threatened to disown her: after all, you can't be a successful politician with a druggie as a daughter, can you?!

"He doesn't care about seeing me, Mom. It's what the courts decided—and a bunch of social workers. Stupid as politicians, and care even less."

"Oh, Christy, what a silly thing to say." She went back into the room and came out running her belt through the loops on her jeans. "He loves you. Why don't you ever want to spend time with him?"

"You know why, Mom," Christy said, realizing at the same time she should have kept her mouth shut.

Her Mom stopped buckling the belt, put her hands on her hips and fixed her with a stern gaze. "When are you going to grow up and quit blaming your problems on everyone else?"

Christy slumped and looked off to her right. *Never, Mom, never. At least not until I'm gone where you can't see me anymore.* She looked back at her Mom. They stood there for a moment, their eyes locked together, then her Mom stirred and finished buckling her belt.

"Honestly, Christy…" She brushed past her. "Listen, I'm going to the store for a couple of things, and then I'm going over to see Paul. Do your homework while I'm gone, and make sure you pack!"

Christy heard her Mom pick her purse up off the coffee table and pull her keys out. "Please try and be mature. It's good for you to spend some time with your Dad."

Yeah, sure, Mom. The only reason you want me to go see Dad is so Paul can come over here and spend the night with you. You won't do it when I'm here because you know what an idiot he is, and how childish it is for you to be sleeping with him.

"Christy? Are you listening to me?!"

Christy turned around and headed into her room. "Yes, Mom, I heard you."

She heard her Mom sigh, then the door opened, keys jingling, and the door slammed shut. *Finally! Some peace and quiet.* She flipped her music on and dropped face down on the bed.

"…number two hit only two years ago," the DJ said, "…haven't heard a thing from that band since! Where do these people disappear to? Nonstop hour of music after this break… stay with us!"

*

Oh, damn, I must've fallen asleep! She raised her head off the bed and blinked at the clock— 11:27. Christy sat up and ran her hands through her hair. Looking down, she saw her homework spread out before her…the pages of the history book all crinkled up from sleeping on them. She laughed at herself and swung her legs around, so she was sitting on the edge of the bed. Wonder if Mom's back yet. I didn't hear her come in if she is. She reached down and untied her shoes, then pulled them off. She pulled off her right sock—

She gasped. Her foot was gone.

There was nothing there—it was gone.

No, wait, it was not gone...she could feel it touching the floor—could feel the carpet against the bottom of her foot. She reached down and grabbed at it—and felt flesh and bone. It was there—but it wasn't there...she couldn't see it. At the bottom of her jeans was—nothing. Was it her eyes? Her vision? No, she could see every-thing else fine.

She ran her fingers over it. She could feel the smooth top of her foot with her thumb, the tougher skin of the soles with her other fingers, and the sensation of her fingers touching her foot. But she couldn't *see* it.

She grabbed the bottom of the pants leg and pulled it up as far as it would go. Her leg was there...right down to the ankle. Then...nothing.

She yanked the left sock off and verified that it was the same as the right. *Am I asleep—crazy —blind—what's happening?!* She jumped up and ran to the mirror on her closet door. Now she could feel her heart pounding against her chest, the hot flush of fear in her cheeks. She looked down at her reflection in the mirror.

It was as if a footless person were floating in just a few inches above the floor. She closed her eyes, shook her head, and looked again. No change…

She became aware that she had been standing there for a while. *Wake up! Do something!* She turned and threw open her door and ran don the hall to her Mom's room. The door was closed, but she flung it open.

"Mom! Mom!"

Her Mom was sitting on the bed with her back towards the door. She turned around and slashed her hand in a flat arc, mouthing the words "*be quiet!*" with so much force it was as if she yelled. She was on the phone. "Mom, I'm —mom, I don't know what's happening—"

Her Mom covered the mouthpiece with her hand. "Christy! Can't you see I'm on the phone! Can't you wait just a minute—and can't you *knock*?!"

"But Mom, I—

"*Shut up*! It can wait—now get out!" She turned back around to the phone, her tone of voice changing as if she flipped a switch, "Sorry, Jane, now what was I saying? Oh, yeah, well, he was telling me about this secretary at his work, and—"

Christy stood dumbfounded for a moment, then turned and went back to her room. Fine, you don't care. Some stupid conversation more important than something bad happening to your only daughter. Fine. I shouldn't have expected anything different anyway—

She closed her door and slouched back down on the bed. *Oh, great, now I'm crying…what am I going to do?*

After a while, she sat up and, without looking, put her socks back on. Her feet felt normal and she couldn't see them. That was better. The clock read 12:59 AM. She switched off the light, and slid in under the covers without bothering to change clothes. *Will I even be able to sleep? Maybe this is a bad dream—I haven't slept much the past week. Maybe I'm hallucinating. Maybe I'm losing my mind. Maybe it was the drugs.* Thoughts drifted in and out, and she fell into a deep sleep.

*

The last bell rang. Christy jumped out of her seat and headed towards the door of the classroom.

"Hey Christy!"

Christy turned around. It was Melinda.

"Do you want to go to the movies tomorrow night with us?"

Christy frowned. "I can't. I'm staying with my Dad all weekend." *Damn. They don't ask me very often, and I'm really tired of being alone.* "Maybe next weekend?"

"I have to baby-sit next Friday and Saturday. Maybe some other time. See you later." She walked out the door.

Christy hung her head, then looked up quickly. "Uh—thanks for asking, Melinda…" But Melinda was already out of hearing range.

Okay, time to go find Dad. She went to her locker, got her books and her duffel bag for the weekend. Thinking of her clothes made her think of what happened last night. Her heart began pounding, just like it did every time she thought of it. This morning, it was the same. She had taken a shower and got dressed without looking down at her feet.

"Christy! Christy!"

It was her Dad. Standing beside the open door of his car, waving at her. She turned and walked to the passenger side and dropped into the seat, her book bag and duffel bag on her legs.

"How have you been?" he asked, getting in and starting the car.

"Fine. Okay, I guess."

"How was school?"

"It was alright."

He was silent as he turned out of the school grounds. It's always so uncomfortable between us. But we both pretend it's not.

"Hey—how about we order pizza tomorrow night and rent a movie? Does that sound good?"

"Sure. Sounds good."

Silence again. He turned onto the freeway ramp and sped up.

"You okay? You look kinda down."

Christy turned and looked at him. He was glancing over at her as he drove. Almost looking like he cares. His brow was furrowed. "Is something wrong?"

Do I tell you what happened last night? I want to tell someone...but...it's too weird. You'd send me away to a counselor, like you did before the divorce. It would end up being my fault, somehow...

"Christy?"

Oh, gosh, I want to tell someone! "Nah—nothing. Just a long week, and I haven't gotten much sleep."

He looked at her for a second as if debating whether to believe her or not, then turned his attention back to driving. Now it was quite uncomfortable. She needed to change the subject because she knew he'd keep prying. "So, what are we going to do tonight?"

Now it was his turn to hesitate. "Um…uh, well, honey, I'm supposed to go out with Cherese tonight. Look, it—"

Her shoulders sagged, and she turned away from him to look out the window. *Of course. Just like Mom. And you don't even see me that often.*

"Look, it just happened. I didn't have any plans, but she has this company get-together, and she really needs to be there, and I just need to go for her." She could feel him looking at the back of her head. "You understand, right? And I got lots of snacks and movies at home for you." Christy nodded without turning her head.

"I'm sorry, Christy." *He really does sound sorry. But it's probably an act.* "Look, Christy, we'll spend all day tomorrow, and we'll do whatever you want." He was trying to be cheerful now. "Anything you want. Okay?"

She sighed. "Okay."

By myself again tonight. Who knows when he'll be home? He left at 4:30, and said he didn't know when he'd be back. She watched TV, did some homework, then began getting ready for bed. She pulled off her pants.

It was up to her knees now.

Oh my gosh, oh gosh, what's happening to me? Oh, God, please stop this, oh please, why…

It was a while before she could get up and wash her face. Then she went into her Dad's bathroom and opened the cupboards. Shaving lotion, toothpaste, old medicine bottle, cough syrup, cold medicine. *Nothing to help me sleep? Wait—the cold medicine.* She took it out and scanned the label. There! CAUTION: MAY CAUSE DROWSINESS. Just what she needed. She didn't bother to get a spoon, just swigged down what she guessed was a little more than the recommended dose.

She sat down on the bed in the guest room. She looked over at the phone sitting on the nightstand. *I need to talk to someone. But who would care?* She picked up the phone and dialed Melinda's number.

"Hello?"

"Hi, Melinda, this is Christy."

"Oh, uh, hi, Christy. Listen—"

"Are you busy right now?"

"Well, actually, I was just leaving, we're—"

Christy felt awkward now, "Oh, I'm sorry. I'll talk to you later."

She hung up quickly. *I could try someone else.* She paced around the room for a while, then snapped up the phone and called Jennifer.

The answering machine came on, and she hung up. She sat down on the bed.

*

She sat at her desk, tapping her pencil on the notebook in front of her. Monday morning. Five more minutes until lunch. She had decided last night that she would try and talk to the school counselor after science class. When the bell rang, she swept up her things and headed down the hall to knock on Mr. DiMuri's office door before she could lose her nerve.

"Come in!" She opened the door and stepped inside, shutting it behind her. Mr. DiMuri was a small, kindly, man. He loved his work, so much so that he never noticed how many of the kids made fun of him because he seemed so oblivious. He just thought they were laughing because they liked him. *How nice it would be to be so oblivious.*

"Hello—Christy is it?" Mr. DiMuri prided himself on remembering students' names. "This is your first year."

"Yes, that's right." How is she going to do this? She rehearsed it over and over, but now it seemed too crazy. *How do I begin? I can't do this.* But she was desperate: this morning it had worsened: she was invisible from the waist down. *If this keeps on, I won't be able to hide it. I have to tell someone. Eventually, I'll be—*

"How can I help you?" She noticed for the first time that he was not sitting at his desk, he was standing and putting papers into a briefcase and straightening things up.

"I was wondering if I could—if I could talk to you for a bit?" Much more timid and quiet than she intended. *He probably thinks I'm retarded.*

"Well, I am getting ready to go to a meeting right now—is it something quick?"

"Oh, no, it's—well, no."

He clicked his briefcase shut. "Well, that's okay. Come back after your classes at 3:00. It's not an emergency, is it?" He smiled as if he had made a joke.

"Oh, no, no."

"Okay, then. I will see you at 3:00." He picked up the briefcase and headed for the door.

She nodded quickly and scooted out of the office. She was nervous, but felt lighter some-how. Maybe this was good—yes, this was good. She could finally tell someone, and could get some help. Mr. DiMuri was a kind man, even if he was a little ditzy.

*

She threaded her way through the mass of people going the other way down the hall. They were all leaving, the building, going home for the day, but she was going back toward the offices.

Standing in front of the closed door to his office, she hesitated. Can I do this? I'm not used to telling people anything personal, or how I feel about things. It usually means they'll hate me eventually. But this is different. Something is wrong with me—something quite strange. What if he doesn't believe me? What if he thinks I'm crazy? Well, I'll show him. Then he'll believe.

She raised her hand to knock on the door, when suddenly the door opened, and Mr. DiMuri, with one arm full of books and keys in the other hand, was coming out. Christy stepped back in surprise. "Oh!"

Mr. DiMuri jumped and looked up, "Oh, my! What—" He looked at her with a frown, then softened. "Oh, we were supposed to meet, weren't we?"

"Yes, sir. I—"

"Oh, I'm sorry. I have an appointment I must get to. My fault, my fault. Can we make it tomorrow? Tomorrow should be fine?" He looked at her questioningly.

"Uh, sure, that will be okay." She could feel that she wasn't hiding the disappointment very well. *Another person who thinks everything is more important than my problems.*

"Well, good. It can wait?"

"Oh, yes, it can wait." I suppose. Everything can wait.

"Good, then," he said. He turned, shut the door, and locked it, "we'll meet tomorrow after school."

Yeah, sure, thought Christy, if I am still around.

*

What a horrible week. And it's only Wednesday. Christy stepped onto the porch of her house. Of course, all of them are bad...but this one is worse than most. No one is interested in me, or cares about me. No one ever says, "how are you doing, Christy?" and means it. They just mean, "hi." They don't want an answer.

She opened the door, and saw her grandmother lumbering out of the kitchen. "Hello, Christy! How are you?"

"Hi, grandma. What are you doing here?"

"Well, *that's* a nice greeting. Your Mom was going to be gone all day working on a project at work, so I told her I'd come over and clean the house for her and make dinner."

"Oh."

"Why are you wearing gloves? Is it a new style for you teenagers these days?" *She tries to be nice, but she is just stupid.* "No, I just like them."

"Well, take them off and help me finish dinner. You can make the salad." She turned and headed back into the kitchen.

Christy put her rucksack on the couch. "No, that's okay."

Her grandmother turned back and looked at her sternly. "Your mom told me you've been very disrespectful lately—or more so than usual, I might add. Now listen, young lady, your Mom works very hard and being a single parent is not easy. Especially with a teenage daughter like you. Now get in her and help me. That's not an unreasonable request!"

"Oh, Grandma, I meant 'no' I'm not taking the gloves off, not—"

"I don't *care* what you meant, Christy! Get in here and help me. And then we'll talk about you being more supportive of your Mom in this difficult time."

You don't know the meaning of difficult time, you old bag. Why don't you stay out of it?!

"Don't look at *me* like that! If your Mom had done that when she was young, I'd have smacked her good. Maybe that's what's wrong with you—not enough *discipline*."

Christy took a deep breath and dropped her head. If only these idiots would listen to someone else for a change.

Her grandmother put her arms on her ample hips and softened a bit. "Oh, Christy, look, I know this is hard for everyone. But your Mom has feelings too. Don't make things so difficult for her. It would have been much easier if she didn't have a daughter, but she does, and you've got to help out. Now come on." She turned and walked back into the kitchen.

Easier if she didn't have a daughter? She turned around and walked out the front door, making sure it slammed good and hard when she left. *There! See, I DO exist. Even if everyone wishes I didn't.*

*

"Christy, what in the world is going on?"

Her mom was standing in the doorway of Christy's bedroom with her hands on her hips.

Now comes the confrontation. Maybe I should try to tell her the truth.

"What's going on, Christy? Why do you treat me, and your grandmother, and everyone like you hate us? What is the problem?"

Okay, here goes. "Mom, I do have a problem. I—"

"Well, finally, you can admit something! You know, you are—"

"Mom! I'm trying to tell you—"

"Christy, you always think the world revolves around you. Well, it doesn't! Other people have problems, too! You have to learn to give, sometimes, too. I have worked hard to raise you and give you things you want, and this is the thanks I receive? What's wrong with you?!"

"Mom, parts of me are—I mean, I seem to be…"

"Look, I understand divorce is hard on children. And me having to work so hard and be gone so much. But this is just the way it is. Divorce and moving aren't easy on me, either, you know! You have to grow up! We have to do this *together*."

"Mom, parts of me are … disappearing." *There! It was done! I said it!*

"Now listen to me. I have to go out now, and I want *you* to clean the kitchen, like I asked you to do when you got home from school. Now please *do* it this time, and show you can be part of this family, hard as that might be!"

Christy sat dumbfounded. *Did she even hear me?* "Mom, I can't—"

"Christy! No more excuses! Just do this one simple thing this one time, and we'll talk about the rest later! Please?!"

Her mom turned and stomped down the hall. *Slam!* Went the door, and the windows in the house shook. Then all was empty and quiet.

She looked down at her gloved hands, and began crying.

After a while, she stood up and walked over to the mirror and looked at her reflection.

But, of course, there was nothing there.

Karma and Santayana

Susanne Perry[1]

Finally, the day had arrived. After forty years of bored students, irrational parents, inept administrators and clueless coworkers, it was my last day in this godforsaken classroom. When I became a teacher all those years ago, it wasn't to have the summers off as some idiot will say, thinking they're so clever. Yeah, ha-ha.

In truth, my motivation was a love of history. I became a history teacher because history was all I wanted to talk about, all I wanted to read

[1]Susanne Perry began writing novels in 2016 and discovered short story writing the following year. Susanne's City Streets series are three mysteries themed in urban issues and set in street communities of the Pacific Northwest. Swan Song, her fourth novel, a thriller about impending death and revenge, was released in February 2023. A voracious reader of crime thrillers, mysteries, and historical fiction, find Susanne at http://susanneperrybooks.com and on LinkedIn and Instagram.

about. I needed a job after college, and I wanted to be involved with something I felt passionate about. But right now, I'm tired, and I don't remember feeling passionate about anything.

There will be the obligatory send-off in the faculty lunchroom, with the usual lame cards and comments. *We're gonna miss you around here, man.* Sure. Right. These clowns will miss me until the moment they raid the shelves in my vacant classroom of supplies, like victors of war reaping the spoils. My fellow teachers aren't gonna miss me any more than I will miss them. Good riddance.

If history taught me anything, and it most definitely has taught me much, it's that people can find immeasurable reserves of strength at times when it's most needed. I could offer points of discussion, but I won't bore you. I'm retiring. My days of boring people with history are coming to an end, and the only immeasurable strength I can relate to is that I showed up to work every day in these last few miserable years.

History, or more correctly, social observation also taught me that when one is of a certain age, one should move aside and let another take the wheel before you become a jaded, ugly caricature of yourself. Unfortunately, we aren't aware of that beast nipping at our heels until it's too late.

As a new teacher, I went home each day covered in chalk dust and excited about classroom discussions. Debates about the Revolutionary War, the Industrial Revolution, the Louisiana Purchase, admission of states to the union—all topics that excited me, and it was gratifying to see them excite my students. It didn't last. Chalk dust was eliminated by a laptop and projector. I didn't miss the chalk dust.

Glancing around the room that I had occupied for most of my career depressed me. The room was absent of any vestige of my influence. Forty damned years, and you would have thought I'd never been there. I turned and walked out with one last box of crap that I would probably stick in the garage at home and never look at again.

I walked to the teacher parking lot, placed the box in the bed of my truck, and turned back to the building. Knowing what awaited me in the staff room, I was tempted to get in my truck and leave, but even I'm not that big of an asshole. And I'd be damned if I'd let them say that I was.

Trudging back into the building, I walked down the corridor and into the staff room. The room was filled with teaching staff and administrators, most of whom I recognized, but not all. I wasn't the only poor sucker heading out the door for good. It didn't surprise me that people unfamiliar to me would be in attendance.

I was only a step inside the room when Carlson, the vice principal, saw me, raised his arms in mock surprise, then clapped his hands together as a signal. "All right, everyone! It's one of our esteemed guests." Carlson's announcement was met with applause, and hands reached out to shake mine. I felt the light slap of palms against my back and shoulders. There was a sneaky quality to Carlson that made me wonder if he was angling for a promotion.

I studied Carlson a moment longer as someone handed me a plastic cup of something. I took a sip. Not bad. I could choke down one drink, endure the banality for a while, and get the hell out of here. I watched Carlson. He was much too motivated for the last day of the school year. Most of us were too exhausted at this point to care.

Carlson stepped over to me and raised his hand to get everyone's attention. With his hand on my shoulder, he said a few things about me, my dedication, the impact we all hoped to have on students. Blah, blah. I wasn't really listening. He was talking about someone I didn't know anymore, someone I used to be.

As Carlson finished speaking and the crowd joined him in applause one more time, he placed a large envelope in my hands. The envelope was not heavy, but full of papers and such. Cards and notes from colleagues, I assumed. Carlson leaned over and said, "For later, when you have more time."

I endured a few brief, mind-numbing conversations, confirming how uninterested I was in being there. These younger teachers were much too excited. I felt a headache coming on. I sipped my drink and looked around for anyone around my age with whom I could stomach a few minutes of small talk. Greenwood, who was retiring from teaching English, was near the door. He turned in my direction, but didn't see me through the crowd. Before I could step in that direction, Greenwood was gone.

Staring into the plastic cup for a few seconds, I saw that it was empty. *When had I finished my drink?* No matter, I thought. I'd pour myself a real drink at home. I dropped the cup into the wastebasket. I shook a couple of hands as I made my way to the door, the envelope from Carlson under my arm, and walked out. Freedom.

My truck was parked next to Greenwood's small hybrid. The front ends of both vehicles were facing in my direction, and Greenwood was sitting behind his steering wheel. As I approached, I lifted my hand in greeting and walked closer. Greenwood hesitated, but then stuck his hand out of the driver's side window and shook my hand.

"Hey, Greenwood," I said. "We're both out of here. We've made it out the other side."

Greenwood nodded. "How many years for you?" he asked. "I've lost count."

"Forty," I answered. "You were here when I started. How many for you?"

"Forty-five," answered Greenwood. "I remember your first day. You were full of new ideas and so motivated," he said, pointing his finger at me. "You were an encouragement to many of us who had already begun to lose our grip. You reminded us that it was about the kids. We had forgotten that. At least I had. I never forgot it again."

I looked at Greenwood. If I hadn't known better, I could have sworn there were tears in his eyes. I was embarrassed by his words but managed to acknowledge the sentiment with a nod and a thank-you.

"Did you?" he asked.

"Did I what?" I asked him. I was confused and must have looked it.

Greenwood shook his head. "Nothing. Just thinking of the old saying, 'Those who cannot remember the past are doomed to repeat it.' Do you remember the saying?"

"Of course. Santayana, am I correct?"

"It's been attributed to him, yes." He smiled with tears in his eyes. Greenwood wiped his face with his hand and said, "Glad to have a chance to wish you the best."

"Same to you, Greenwood." I rapped a knuckle on his car door as a goodbye. He backed out and drove away.

I watched the hybrid drive off, offering one last wave, and ambled over to my truck. As I sat down in the front seat, I placed Carlson's envelope on the passenger seat and rested my hands on the steering wheel. I looked at the envelope and considered looking through a few of the notes, but decided they would keep. I glanced over at the doorway to the building; I had not seen another faculty member leave the party. How they could stand hanging out this long was beyond me.

The events of the day caught up with me and fatigue set in. I wasn't a young person any longer and was tired after a full day of teaching. I admitted to myself that I was exhausted. Totally wiped out. I took a deep breath and decided to rest for a few minutes, a quick detox to rid my system of the day.

I woke with a jolt; dazed, disoriented, and not realizing that I'd dozed off. The vehicle I sat in was not my own. Wait, yes it was…well, it had been at one time. It took a few moments for me to place the dashboard of the Chevy, the car I drove in college. I took a deep breath. I was dreaming, that was all.

The building itself had changed. The entrance was different. The double door was a deeper color, a color I recognized but hadn't seen in ages. The sun angle told me it was early in the morning. I watched people heading into the building instead of coming out. If I wasn't dreaming, I was in shock caused by the major life change of beginning my retirement. Or someone slipped me a mickey. What a mean prank to pull.

I saw the envelope sitting on the seat next to me and reached for it. Opening the flap, I removed a handful of papers. Then I looked at my palms and saw traces of chalk dust. I wiped them on my jacket, a jacket I hadn't worn in decades. The top sheet of paper was a schedule of meetings. The schedule was headed by a welcome to the new school year. A special welcome was extended to new teachers and my name was listed. The schedule was dated early September forty years prior. I looked in the rearview mirror and gasped as my younger self stared back.

With a shaky hand, I opened the door and stepped out of the Chevy. Nausea hit, and I broke out in a sweat when I saw Cummings, the principal who hired me to teach history. He was standing at the entrance to the building. Cummings saw me and waved me over. The man had been dead for over twenty years. Damn. Greenwood was right; I should have believed Santayana.

About the Riversong Short Story Contest

The Riversong Short Story Contest seeks to highlight unique voices in the short story genre, as well as a place for new and up-and-coming writers to showcase their talent in publication.

The contest runs year around, with the collection of winners published in July or August of each year:

- Deadline: May 15 each year

- Word limit: 10,000 words

- Genre and style: Any except erotica.

- Entry fee: $25

- Winners announced June 15

You may submit your story any time during the year—submissions after May 15 will be scheduled for the next year's contest.

Your manuscript will be reviewed by a panel of editors, bloggers, writers, and publishers. It is a blind review, based solely on content and writing style. Uniqueness of story, voice, plot , and literary skill will make your story stand out. All winners will be contacted privately, and their story will be published in a volume of short stories in the third quarter of each year.

For more, and to enter the contest, visit https://sulisinternational.com/short-story-contest-landing/

About the Publisher

Sulis International Press publishes select fiction and nonfiction in a variety of genres under four imprints: Riversong Books, Sulis Academic Press, Sulis Press, and Keledei Publications.

For more, visit the website at
https://sulisinternational.com

Subscribe to the newsletter at
https://sulisinternational.com/subscribe/

Follow on social media
https://www.facebook.com/SulisInternational
https://twitter.com/Sulis_Intl
https://www.pinterest.com/Sulis_Intl/
https://www.instagram.com/sulis_international/